A Christmas Carol

Copyright © 1986 Victoria House Publishing Ltd

Produced for Blackie and Son Limited by Victoria
House Publishing Ltd

British Library Cataloguing in Publication Data
Dickens, Charles, *1812–1870*
    A Christmas carol.
    I. Title   II. Worsley, John
    823′ .8   PR4572.C68

    ISBN 0–216–92080–9

Blackie and Son Limited
7 Leicester Place
LONDON WC2H 7BP

Printed in Hong Kong

Charles Dickens
A CHRISTMAS CAROL

Illustrated by John Worsley

Adapted by Jane Wilton-Smith

Blackie

Contents

MARLEY'S GHOST

Marley was dead, to begin with. There is no doubt whatever about that. The register of his burial was signed by the clergyman, the clerk, the undertaker, and the chief mourner. Scrooge signed it.

Old Marley was as dead as a door-nail.

Scrooge knew he was dead? Of course he did. How could it be otherwise? Scrooge and Marley were partners for I don't know how many years.

No. There is no doubt that Marley was dead. This must be distinctly understood, or nothing wonderful can come of the story I am going to tell you.

Scrooge never painted out Old Marley's name. There it stood, years afterwards, above the warehouse door. Scrooge and Marley. The firm was known as Scrooge and Marley. Sometimes people called Scrooge, Scrooge, and sometimes Marley, but he answered to both names. It was all the same to him.

Oh! but he was a tight-fisted hand at the grindstone. Scrooge! A squeezing, wrenching, grasping, scraping, clutching, covetous old sinner! Nobody ever stopped him in the street to say, 'My dear Scrooge, how are you? When will you come to see me?' But what did Scrooge care! He liked to be left alone. The better to go about his business.

Once upon a time—of all the good days in the year, on Christmas Eve—old Scrooge sat busy in his counting-house. It was cold, bleak, biting weather. The city clocks had only just gone three, but it was quite dark already.

The door of Scrooge's counting-house was open so that he could see his clerk, Bob Cratchit, who was copying letters in a dismal little room. Scrooge had a very small fire going, but the clerk's fire was so very much smaller that it looked like one coal. But Bob Cratchit couldn't refill it, for Scrooge kept the coal box in his own room. So the clerk put on his white

scarf, and tried to warm himself at the candle—and of course he failed.

'A merry Christmas, Uncle! God save you!' cried a cheerful voice. It was the voice of Scrooge's nephew, Fred.

'Bah!' said Scrooge. 'Humbug!'

'Christmas a humbug, Uncle!' said Scrooge's nephew. 'You don't mean that, I am sure!'

'I do,' said Scrooge. 'Merry Christmas! Bah!'

'Don't be cross, Uncle!' said the nephew.

'What else can I be,' returned the uncle, 'when I live in such a world of fools as this? Merry Christmas indeed! What's Christmas time to you but a time for paying bills without money; a time for finding yourself a year older, but not an hour richer.'

'Uncle!' pleaded the nephew.

'Nephew!' answered the uncle, sternly, 'keep Christmas in your own way, and let me keep it in mine.'

'Keep it!' repeated Scrooge's nephew. 'But you don't do anything for it!'

'Let me have it alone, then,' said Scrooge.

'Don't be angry, Uncle. Come! Dine with us tomorrow.'

'Good afternoon!' said Scrooge, ignoring the invitation. His nephew left the room without an angry word, and as he left two other gentlemen came in.

'At this festive season of the year, Mr Scrooge,' said one of the gentlemen, 'a few of us are trying to raise money to buy the poor some meat and drink, and means of warmth.'

'Are there no prisons? Are there no workhouses?' growled Scrooge.

'Many can't go there; and many would rather die.'

'If they would rather die,' said Scrooge, 'they had better do it, and decrease the surplus population. Leave more room for the rest of us.'

Seeing clearly that it would be useless to ask Scrooge for money, the gentlemen left. Scrooge went back to his work, feeling pleased with himself.

At length, the hour of shutting up the counting-house arrived and Scrooge went home. He lived on his own in a dank, gloomy building. The front door had a knocker that Scrooge had seen every night and every morning for many years. Now there was nothing at all particular about this knocker, except that it was very large. So how was it that when Scrooge put his key in the lock of the door, he saw not a knocker, but Marley's face?

Marley's face. It was not angry or ferocious, but looked at Scrooge as Marley used to look. Then, while Scrooge stared at it, it was a knocker again.

To say that he was not startled would be untrue. He opened

the door, entered and then locked it firmly behind him. He was not a man to be easily frightened, but he did look round to make sure that all was right.

Sitting-room, bedroom, lumber-room. All as they should be. Nobody under the table, nobody under the sofa; a small fire in the grate; spoon and basin ready; and the little saucepan of gruel upon the hob. Nobody under the bed; nobody in his dressing-gown, which was hanging against the wall.

Quite satisfied, Scrooge closed his door, and locked himself in. Then he took off his cravat, put on his dressing-gown and slippers, and his nightcap, and sat down before the fire to take his gruel. As he did so, his glance happened to rest upon a bell,

a disused bell, that hung in the room. With great astonishment he saw this bell begin to swing. It swung so softly at first that it scarcely made a sound; but soon it rang loudly, and so did every bell in the house.

Suddenly the bells ceased and a clanking noise started, as if someone were dragging a heavy chain. Scrooge heard the noise coming nearer to him until it came into the room through the heavy door. It was Marley's ghost!

The same face: the very same. Marley in his pigtail, usual waistcoat, tights and boots. The chain he dragged was fastened round his middle. It was long, and wound about him like a tail.

'Who are you?' asked Scrooge.

'Ask me who I *was*.'

'Who *were* you then?' asked Scrooge, raising his voice.

'In life I was your partner, Jacob Marley.'

'You are chained,' said Scrooge, trembling. 'Tell me why?'

'I wear the chain I forged in life,' replied the ghost. 'You have forged one for yourself already.'

'Jacob,' said Scrooge, imploringly. 'Old Jacob Marley, tell me more and comfort me, Jacob!'

'I am here tonight to warn you that you have a chance of escaping my fate. I can help you in that, Ebenezer.'

'Thank'ee good friend,' said Scrooge.

'You will be haunted,' went on the ghost, 'by three spirits.'

Scrooge's face fell. 'Is that the chance you mentioned, Jacob?'

'It is.'

'I—I think I'd rather not,' said Scrooge.

'You cannot escape my fate without them,' said the ghost. 'Expect the first tomorrow, when the bell tolls one. Expect the second on the next night at one and the third on the following night at one. You will not see me again, but remember what I have said.'

When it had said these words, the spectre walked slowly towards the window, dragging its chain behind. With one arm raised in farewell, it passed clean through the window, and floated out into the bleak, dark night. Scrooge examined the door by which the ghost had entered. It was still locked, as he

had locked it with his own hands, and the bolts were undisturbed. Had he seen Marley's ghost in a dream? He was too tired to think. He went to bed and fell asleep straight away.

THE FIRST OF
THE THREE SPIRITS

Scrooge awoke to the chimes of a neighbouring church. It was so dark that he listened for the hour. To his great surprise the heavy bell chimed twelve. Twelve! It had been past two when he went to bed. The clock was wrong. An icicle must have got into the works. Twelve.

'Why, it isn't possible,' said Scrooge, 'that I can have slept through a whole day and far into another night. It isn't possible that anything has happened to the sun, and this is twelve noon!'

This idea alarmed him, so he scrambled out of bed and groped his way to the window. All he could make out was that it was still very foggy and extremely cold.

Scrooge went to bed again, and thought, and thought, and thought, and could make nothing of it. The more he thought, the more puzzled he was; and the more he tried not to think, the more he thought. Marley's ghost bothered him very much. Was it a dream or not?

Scrooge lay like this until the clock chimed a quarter to one. Then he remembered that the ghost had warned him of a visitation when the bell tolled one. At length the clock chimed again.

'Ding, dong!'

'A quarter past,' said Scrooge, counting.

'Ding, dong!'

'Half-past!' said Scrooge.

'Ding, dong!'

'A quarter to the hour,' said Scrooge.

'Ding, dong!'

'The hour itself,' said Scrooge, triumphantly, 'and nothing else!'

He spoke before the hour bell sounded, which it now did with a deep, dull, hollow *one*.

Light flashed up in the room and the curtains of his bed were drawn. The curtains of his bed were drawn aside, I tell you, by a hand, and Scrooge found himself face to face with the unearthly visitor who had drawn them. It was a strange figure —like a child and like an old man, all at once. The strangest thing about it was a bright light that sprung from the crown of its head. And it held a great cap under its arm.

'Are you the spirit, sir, whose coming was foretold to me?' asked Scrooge.

'I am!' said the spirit.

'Who, and what are you?' Scrooge demanded.

'I am the Ghost of Christmas Past. Your past.'

'What has brought you here?' asked Scrooge.

'Your welfare!' said the ghost. It put out its strong hand as it spoke, and clasped him gently by the arm. 'Rise! and walk with me!'

As the words were spoken, they passed through the

bedroom wall, and stood on an open country road, with fields on either side. The city, the darkness and the fog had entirely vanished.

'Good Heavens!' said Scrooge, clasping his hands together, as he looked around him. 'I was loved in this place. I was a boy here!'

They walked along the road, Scrooge recognizing every gate, and post, and tree. Some boys were playing in the fields, laughing and shouting to each other.

'These are but shadows of the things that have been,' said the ghost. 'They have no consciousness of us.'

As they came nearer, Scrooge recognized every one of them. Why was he so glad when he heard them wish each other

'Merry Christmas' as they went home? What was 'Merry Christmas' to Scrooge? What good had it ever done to him?

'The school is not quite deserted,' said the ghost. 'A solitary child, neglected by his friends, is left there still.'

Scrooge said he knew it. And he sobbed.

They soon came to the school and went into a long, bare room, full of desks. At one of these a lonely boy was reading near a feeble fire; and Scrooge sat down upon a seat and wept to see his poor forgotten self as he used to be.

'Poor boy,' exclaimed Scrooge, and cried again.

'I wish—' he muttered, drying his eyes with his cuff, 'but it's too late now.'

'What is the matter?' asked the spirit.

'Nothing,' said Scrooge. 'There was a boy singing a Christmas carol at my door last night. I should like to have given him something; that's all.'

The ghost smiled thoughtfully and said, 'Let us see another Christmas!'

Straight away they were in a busy street outside a warehouse door. They went in. An old gentleman was sitting behind a high desk.

Scrooge cried in great excitement: 'Why it's Fezziwig, my old master!'

Old Fezziwig laid down his pen, rubbed his hands and called out in a jovial voice: 'Yo ho there, Ebenezer!'

Scrooge's former self, now grown a young man, came briskly in.

'No more work tonight. It's Christmas Eve. Clear away and let's have lots of room here!' said Fezziwig. The young Scrooge cleared away and in came a fiddler. In came Mrs Fezziwig and the three Miss Fezziwigs, beaming and lovable. In came all the young men and women employed in the business, and lots of other people who all danced and laughed and wished each other 'Merry Christmas'.

When the clock struck eleven, this domestic ball broke up. Mr Fezziwig shook hands with every person as he or she went out, and wished him or her 'Merry Christmas'.

Scrooge saw that by this cheerfulness, Old Fezziwig had given a lot of happiness to the people who worked for him. The ghost knew what he was thinking.

'What is the matter?' it asked.

'Nothing particular,' said Scrooge.

'Something, I think?' the ghost insisted.

'No,' said Scrooge. 'No. I should like to be able to say a word or two to my clerk just now. That's all.'

Again the scene changed and Scrooge saw himself as a man in the prime of his life. He was not alone but he stood by the side of a fair young girl with tears in her eyes.

'It matters little,' she said softly, 'that you no longer love me as you used to when we were both poor. We used to be happy then. But now money is more important to you. Knowing this, I will not hold you to your promise to marry me. We shall part. May you be happy in the life you have chosen!'

She left him and they parted.

'Spirit!' said Scrooge, 'show me no more! Take me home. Why do you delight to torture me?'

'One shadow more!' exclaimed the ghost.

'No more!' cried Scrooge. 'I don't wish to see it!'

But the relentless ghost held him by both arms, and forced

him to see what happened next.

They were in a different room where there was a beautiful little girl playing with many other children. The girl's mother was there too, and Scrooge saw that she was the young lady of the last scene, now grown older.

Scrooge looked on more attentively than ever, when the master of the house walked into the room. The children all rushed to greet him. If Scrooge had married he might have been in this lucky man's place.

'Spirit!' said Scrooge, in a broken voice, 'remove me from this place.'

'I told you these were shadows of the things that have been,' said the ghost. 'That they are what they are, do not blame me.'

'Remove me!' Scrooge exclaimed, 'I cannot bear it! Leave me! Take me back. Haunt me no longer!'

Scrooge seized the spirit's cap and pressed it down upon its head to try to put out the light that shone from it. But still the light shone . . .

Scrooge was back in his bedroom, in his bed, and fast asleep.

THE SECOND OF
THE THREE SPIRITS

The next night, when he awoke in the middle of a snore and sat up in bed to get his thoughts together, Scrooge did not need to be told that the bell was again striking one. His room was flooded with light, which seemed to stream down onto his

bed. As he lay wondering what would happen, he thought that perhaps this ghostly light was coming from the next room. So he got up softly and shuffled in his slippers to the door.

The moment Scrooge's hand was on the lock, a strange voice called him by his name, and asked him to enter. He obeyed.

It was his own room. There was no doubt about that. But it

had changed. The walls and ceiling were hung with Christmas decorations and a great fire had been lit in the hearth. Heaped up on the floor, to form a kind of throne, were turkeys, geese, game, poultry, brawn, great joints of meat, suckling-pigs, long wreaths of sausages, mince pies, plum-puddings, barrels of oysters, red-hot chestnuts, cherry-cheeked apples, juicy oranges, luscious pears and seething bowls of punch. On top of this pile sat a jolly giant. He held up a glowing torch to shed its light on Scrooge as he peeped round the door.

'Come in,' exclaimed the ghost. 'Come in! and know me better, man! I am the Ghost of Christmas Present,' said the spirit. 'Look upon me!'

Scrooge did so timidly. The spirit was clothed in one simple green robe bordered with white fur. Its feet, which Scrooge could see beneath the green robe, were bare; and on its head it wore a holly wreath with shining icicles in it.

'You have never seen the like of me before!' exclaimed the spirit.

'Never,' Scrooge replied.

The Ghost of Christmas Present rose.

'Spirit,' said Scrooge, submissively, 'take me where you will. I was forced to go out last night and I learnt a lesson which is working now. Tonight, if you have anything to teach me, do so.'

'Touch my robe!' commanded the spirit.

Scrooge did as he was told, and held it tight. At once they were standing in the city streets on Christmas morning. People

were scraping snow from the pavement in front of their houses and from the tops of their houses. Others were carrying their dinners to the bakers' shops. The spirit was very interested in this and he stood with Scrooge beside him, sprinkling incense from his torch on the dinners. This seemed to make people who were about to quarrel become friendly with each other. For, they said, it was a shame to quarrel upon Christmas Day. And so it was! God love it, so it was!

Then the spirit went to Scrooge's clerk's home and took Scrooge with him. And he sprinkled incense from his torch on Bob Cratchit's house. Think of that! The Ghost of Christmas Present blessed Bob Cratchit's four-roomed house!

Up rose Mrs Cratchit, Cratchit's wife, dressed in an old dress that she had brightened up with cheap ribbons. She laid the table. Two small Cratchits, boy and girl, came tearing in, shouting that outside the baker's they had smelt the goose, and known it was theirs.

'Whatever is keeping your precious father then?' said Mrs Cratchit. 'And your brother Tiny Tim! And Martha wasn't as late last Christmas Day!'

'Here's Martha, mother!' said a girl, appearing as she spoke.

'Here's Martha, mother!' cried the two young Cratchits. 'Hurrah! There's *such* a goose, Martha!'

'Why bless your heart alive, my dear, how late you are!' said Mrs Cratchit, kissing her a dozen times, and taking off her shawl and bonnet for her. 'But never mind so long as you are come,' she smiled. 'Sit down before the fire, my dear, and have a warm.'

'No, no! There's father coming,' cried the two young Cratchits, who were everywhere at once. 'Hide, Martha!'

So Martha hid herself, and in came Bob, the father. After him came Tiny Tim, who leaned on a little crutch because his legs were supported by an iron frame.

'Why, where's our Martha?' cried Bob Cratchit, looking round.

'Not coming,' said Mrs Cratchit.

'Not coming!' said Bob, very disappointed. 'Not coming on Christmas Day!'

Martha didn't like to play tricks on him so she came out from behind the closet door, and ran into his arms. Then Bob went out to fetch the goose from the baker's, with which he soon returned.

Mrs Cratchit made the gravy hissing hot; Martha dusted the hot plates; Bob took Tiny Tim beside him in a tiny corner at the table; and the two young Cratchits set chairs for everybody. At last the dishes were brought and grace was said. Mrs Cratchit carved.

There never was such a goose. Bob said he didn't believe there ever was such a goose cooked! When that was eaten, in came the pudding. Oh, a wonderful pudding! Blazing in flaming brandy, and with Christmas holly stuck in the top.

At last the pudding was all done and all the Cratchit family drew round the hearth. Bob said: 'A merry Christmas to us all, my dears. God bless us!' Which all the family echoed.

'God bless us every one!' said Tiny Tim, the last of all.

'Spirit,' said Scrooge, with an interest he had never felt before, 'tell me if Tiny Tim will live.'

'I see an empty seat,' replied the ghost, 'in the poor chimney corner, and a crutch without an owner. If nothing happens to change this, the child will die.'

'No, no, spirit!' said Scrooge, 'say he will be spared.'

'If nothing happens to change this, the child will die,' repeated the ghost. 'What then? If he is likely to die, he had better do it, and decrease the surplus population. Leave more room for the rest of us.'

Scrooge hung his head to hear his own words quoted by the spirit, and was overcome with penitence and grief.

The scene changed many times after that as the ghost took Scrooge off to visit hospitals, jails and other places where people had unhappy lives. It was strange that wherever the Spirit of Christmas went, people seemed to become happy. It was strange too, that during this one night the ghost grew older, clearly older. Its hair had become grey.

'Are spirits' lives so short?' asked Scrooge.

'My life upon this globe ends tonight,' replied the ghost.

'Tonight!' cried Scrooge.

'Tonight at midnight. Hark! The time is drawing near.'

The chimes were ringing the three quarters past eleven at that moment.

'Forgive me,' said Scrooge, looking intently at the spirit's robe, 'but I see something strange under your robe. What is it?'

'Look here,' was the spirit's sorrowful reply. It brought two children out from under its robe; wretched, abject, frightful, hideous, miserable. They were a boy and a girl.

'Spirit! Are they yours?' Scrooge cried. 'Have they no refuge or resource?'

'Are there no prisons?' said the spirit, turning on him for the last time with his own words. 'Are there no workhouses?' The bell struck twelve.

Scrooge looked about him for the ghost, and did not see it. As the last stroke ended he remembered Jacob Marley's words. Lifting up his eyes he saw a solemn phantom, draped and hooded, coming, like a mist along the ground, towards him.

THE LAST OF
THE SPIRITS

The phantom slowly, gravely, silently approached. When it came near him, Scrooge bent down on his knee. The spirit was hidden in a deep black mist, so that only one outstretched hand could be seen. The spirit neither spoke nor moved. It filled Scrooge with a solemn dread.

'Am I in the presence of the Ghost of Christmas Yet To Come?' said Scrooge.

The spirit did not answer, but merely pointed.

'You are about to show me shadows of things that have

not happened, but will happen in the time before us,' Scrooge went on. 'Is that so, spirit?'

Still the spirit did not speak.

'Ghost of the future!' exclaimed Scrooge. 'I fear you more than any spectre I have seen. But as I know your purpose is to do me good, I shall stay with you. Will you not speak?'

It gave no reply. The hand pointed straight before them.

'Lead on!' said Scrooge. 'Lead on, spirit!'

The phantom moved away, Scrooge following, and the city seemed to spring up around them. The spirit stopped beside one little knot of businessmen.

The hand pointed to them, so Scrooge listened to their talk.

'When did he die?' inquired one.

'Last night, I believe,' said a great fat man.

'What has he done with his money?' asked a red-faced gentleman.

'I haven't heard,' said the fat man. 'He hasn't left it to *me*. That's all I know.'

The businessmen all laughed. Scrooge knew the men, and looked towards the spirit for an explanation. It did not speak but glided on into a street in a very low, ugly part of the town, where Scrooge had never been before.

They entered a filthy shop where a ragged old man sat, smoking a pipe. At the same time a woman with a heavy

bundle slunk into the shop. Then another woman with a bundle came in too; she was closely followed by a man in faded black.

'Look here, Old Joe,' said the first woman. 'Look what we've brought.'

'Come into the parlour,' said Old Joe, taking the pipe from his mouth. 'Come into the parlour and we'll have a look.'

The parlour was simply a space at the back of the shop. It was just as filthy as the rest of the shop. Old Joe poked the fire and sat down.

'Now then, who's first?' said Old Joe, and the man in faded black produced his small bundle. He had a pencil-case, a pair of cuff links, and a brooch of no great value.

Old Joe looked at them and chalked the sums he was

planning to give for each upon the wall, and added them up
into a total when he found there was nothing more to come.
'That's as much as you'll get from me for those,' said Joe.
'Who's next?'

Mrs Dilber, the woman who had come in second, was next.
She had sheets and towels, a few clothes, two old-fashioned
silver teaspoons, a pair of sugar-tongs, and two pairs of boots.
Old Joe chalked up the prices on the wall in the same way.

'And now undo *my* bundle, Joe,' said the first woman. Joe
went down on his knees to open a sack tied up with string.
He unfastened a great many knots, and dragged out a large
and heavy roll of some dark stuff.

'What do you call this?' said Joe. 'Bed curtains!'

'Ah!' replied the woman, laughing and leaning forward on her crossed arms. 'Bed curtains!'

'You don't mean to say you took these things down, rings and all, with him lying there?' said Joe.

'Yes, I do,' replied the woman. 'Why not?'

'You were born to make your fortune,' said Joe, 'and you'll certainly do it.'

Then the woman held up the best prize of all, a fine shirt.

'Ah! You may look through that shirt till your eyes ache,' she said, 'but you won't find a hole in it, nor a threadbare place. It's the best he had and a fine one too. They'd have wasted it, if it hadn't been for me.'

'What do you call wasting of it?' asked the old man.

'Putting it on him to be buried in, to be sure,' replied the woman with a laugh. 'Somebody was fool enough to do it, but I took it off again. I put an old calico one on him instead.'

Scrooge listened to this dialogue in horror.

'Ha, ha!' laughed the woman, when the old man produced a flannel bag with money in it, to pay for the things they had brought. 'This is the end of it, you see! He frightened everyone away from him when he was alive, to profit us when he was dead! Ha, ha, ha!'

'Spirit!' said Scrooge, shuddering from head to foot. 'I see, I see. The case of this unhappy man might be my own. Spirit, if there is any person in the town who feels emotion caused by this man's death, show that person to me!'

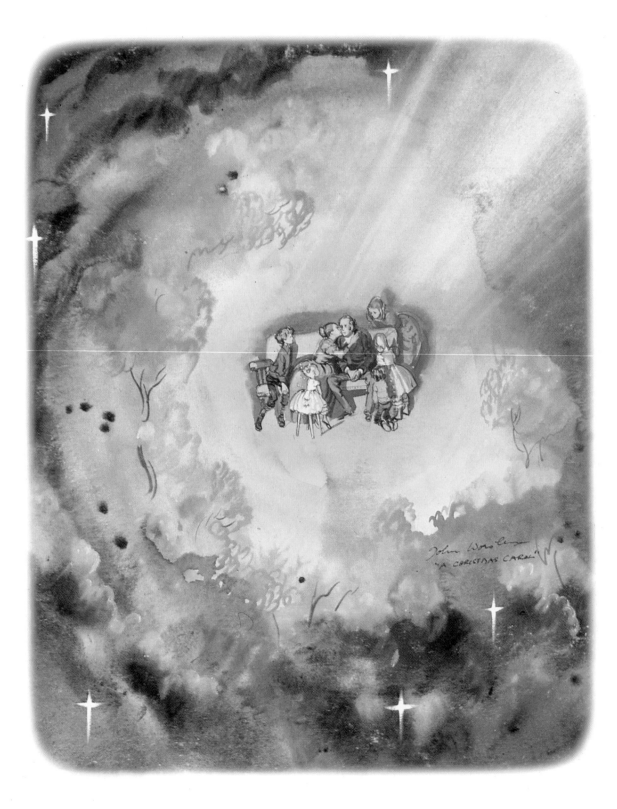

In a second the spirit showed Scrooge a room where a mother and her children sat.

She was anxiously expecting someone, for every few minutes she got up and walked around the room. She would jump at every sound, look out the window, then glance at the clock. She tried, without success, to sew with her needle, but could hardly stand to hear her children's voices while they played.

After a time, the long-expected knock was heard. She hurried to the door, and met her husband. His face was worried and old-looking, although he was a young man.

He came in and sat down to the dinner that had been kept warm for him. After a long silence she asked him, 'Is it good news—or bad?' He seemed embarrassed how to answer.

'Bad,' he answered.

'We are quite ruined?'

'No, there is hope yet, Caroline. He is dead.'

'Thank the Lord for that!' cried the woman, and then, 'Oh, may God forgive me! I was thinking of the money we owe him. To whom shall we owe it now?'

'I don't know,' replied the husband, 'but soon we shall be ready with the money. We may sleep tonight with light hearts, Caroline!'

Yes. It was a happier house for this man's death! The only emotion that the spirit could show Scrooge, caused by the event, was one of pleasure.

Then the spirit led Scrooge to a churchyard. Here the wretched man, whose death he had heard about tonight, lay underneath the ground. He would find out his name.

The spirit stood among the graves, and pointed down to one. Scrooge crept towards it, trembling as he went; and following the finger, read upon the stone of the neglected grave his own name, EBENEZER SCROOGE.

'Am *I* that man whose death I have heard of tonight?' he cried, upon his knees.

The finger pointed from the grave to him, and back again.

'No, Spirit! Oh, no, no!'

The finger was still there.

'Spirit!' he cried, 'hear me! I am not the man I was. I will

honour Christmas in my heart, and try to keep it all the year. I will live in the past, the present, and the future. The spirits of all three shall strive within me. I will not shut out the lessons that they teach. Oh, tell me I may wipe away the writing on this stone!'

In his agony, he caught the spirit's hand. As he clutched it, its hood and dress shrunk, collapsed and dwindled down into a bedpost.

THE END OF IT

Yes! and the bedpost was his own. The bed was his own, the room was his own. Best and happiest of all, the time before him was his own, to make amends in!

'I will live in the past, the present, and the future!' Scrooge repeated, as he scrambled out of his bed.

'Oh, Jacob Marley! Heaven and the Christmas Time be praised for this! I say it on my knees, old Jacob, on my knees!'

His mind was in such a whirl that his voice could hardly say what he wanted it to. He had been sobbing violently when he was in the graveyard with the spirit, and his face was wet with tears. Now he sat on the edge of the bed.

'They are not torn down!' he cried, folding one of his bed curtains in his arms. 'No, they are not torn down, my rings are still here. They are here—I am here—the shadows of the things that would have happened if I carried on in the same old way will disappear. They will. I know they will!'

His hands were busy with his clothes all this time; turning them inside out, putting them on upside-down, tearing them, doing all sorts of silly things.

'I don't know what to do!' cried Scrooge, laughing and crying in the same breath. 'I am as light as a feather, I am as happy as an angel, I am as merry as a schoolboy. I am as giddy as a drunken man. Merry Christmas to everybody! A Happy New Year to all the world! Hallo there! Whoop! Hallo!'

He had frisked into the sitting-room, and was now standing there out of breath.

'There's the saucepan that the gruel was in!' he cried. 'There's the door, by which the ghost of Jacob Marley entered! There's the corner where the Ghost of Christmas Present sat! There's the window where I saw the wandering spirits! It's all right, it's all true, it all happened. Ha, ha, ha!'

Really, for a man who had been out of practice for so many years, it was a splendid laugh.

'I don't know what day of the month it is!' said Scrooge. 'I don't know how long I've been among the spirits. I'm quite a baby. Never mind. I don't care. Hallo! Whoop! Hallo there!'

Running to the window, he opened it, and put out his head. No fog, no mist. A bright, cold day. Oh, glorious!

'What's today?' cried Scrooge, calling down to a boy in Sunday clothes.

'Today!' replied the boy in wonder. 'Why, *Christmas Day*.'

'It's Christmas Day!' said Scrooge to himself. 'I haven't missed it. The spirits have done it all in one night. They can do anything they like. Of course they can.'

'Do you know the butcher's, my fine fellow, in the next street but one,' Scrooge inquired.

'I should hope I did,' replied the lad.

'An intelligent boy!' said Scrooge. 'A remarkable boy! Do you know whether they've sold the prize turkey that was hanging up there?'

'What, the one as big as me?' returned the boy.

'Yes, my buck!'

'It's hanging there now,' replied the boy.

'Is it?' said Scrooge. 'Go and buy it.'

'I don't have that much money!' exclaimed the boy.

'No, no,' said Scrooge. 'Go and buy it for me. Tell 'em to bring it here, so I may explain where to take it. Come back soon, and I'll give you a shilling. Come back in less than five minutes and I'll give you half-a-crown!'

The boy was off like a shot.

'I'll send it to Bob Cratchit's!' whispered Scrooge, rubbing his hands and splitting with a laugh. 'He won't know who sent it. It's twice the size of Tiny Tim.'

His hand was shaking so much that it was very difficult for him to write out Bob Cratchit's address for the butcher. But he

did it somehow. Then he went downstairs to open the door and wait for the turkey to arrive. As he did so the door knocker caught his eye.

'I shall love it as long as I live!' cried Scrooge, patting it with his hand. 'I hardly ever looked at it before. What an honest expression it has in its face! It's a wonderful knocker—Here's the turkey. Hello! How are you! Merry Christmas! What an enormous turkey!'

'Why, it's impossible to carry that to Bob Cratchit's!' said Scrooge to the man who had brought it. 'You must have a cab.'

He chuckled as he said this, he chuckled as he paid the butcher for the turkey, he chuckled as he paid the boy who had run to the shop. What a change had come over Scrooge!

After the turkey was sent Scrooge dressed himself 'all in his best', and went out into the streets. Walking with his hands behind him, he looked at everyone with a delightful smile.

He had not gone far when he saw the gentleman who had asked him for money for the poor. Scrooge immediately took a purse from his pocket and begged the gentleman to accept it.

'My dear sir,' said the gentleman, shaking hands with him. 'I don't know what to say to such munifi—'

'Don't say anything, please,' retorted Scrooge, and walked on to his nephew's house.

He walked past the door a dozen times before he had the courage to go up and knock. But he did it.

'Is your master at home, my dear?' said Scrooge to the maid

who answered the door.

'Yes, sir.'

'Where is he?' said Scrooge.

'He's in the dining-room, sir. Let me show you in.'

'Thank'ee. He knows me,' said Scrooge, with his hand already on the handle of the dining-room door. 'I'll go in, my dear.'

He turned it gently and peeped round the door.

'Fred,' said Scrooge.

Dear heart alive, how his niece by marriage (Fred's wife) started! 'Why bless my soul!' cried Fred. 'Who's that?'

'It's I. Your Uncle Scrooge. I have come to dinner. Will you let me in, Fred?'

Let him in! It is a mercy he didn't shake his arm off. Scrooge was at home in five minutes. Wonderful party, wonderful games, wonderful togetherness, won-der-ful happiness!

But he was early at the office next morning. If he could only be there first, and catch Bob Cratchit coming late!

The clock struck nine. No Bob. A quarter past. No Bob. And he did it; yes, he did! He was full eighteen minutes and a half behind his time.

'Hello!' growled Scrooge. 'What do you mean by coming in at this time of day?'

'I am very sorry, sir,' said Bob. 'I *am* very late today.'

'You are?' said Scrooge. 'Yes. I think you are. Step this way, sir, if you please.'

'It's only once a year, sir,' pleaded Bob. 'It shall not be repeated. I was making rather merry yesterday, sir.'

'Now, I'll tell you what, my friend,' said Scrooge, 'I am not going to stand this sort of thing any longer. And therefore,' he continued, leaping from his stool, 'and therefore I am about to raise your salary!' Bob trembled and looked about him for the ruler. For a moment he thought of knocking Scrooge down with it, holding him, and calling out to all the people in the street outside for help.

'A merry Christmas, Bob!' said Scrooge, clapping him on the back. 'A merrier Christmas, Bob, my good fellow, than I have given you for many a year! I'll raise your salary and assist your struggling family, and we will discuss your affairs over a

cup of Christmas tea!'

In the years to come Scrooge became a second father to Tiny Tim, who did not die. He became as good a friend, as good a master, and as good a man, as the good old city knew, or any other good old city or town knew, in the good old world.

Some people laughed to see the change in him, but he didn't care. His own heart laughed, and that was enough.

At any rate, it was always said of him afterwards, that he knew how to keep Christmas well. May that be truly said of all of us! And so, as Tiny Tim said, God bless us every one!

The End